First published in 2009 in Great Britain by
Barrington Stoke Ltd
18 Walker Street, Edinburgh, EH3 7LP

www.barringtonstoke.co.uk

ISBN: 978-1-84299-710-9

Printed in Great Britain by Bell & Bain Ltd

2 DIE 4

by

Nigel Hinton

A Note from the Author

Have you ever had a phone call where you know someone is there but they don't say a word? It can be very scary if it happens again and again. Who's there? Why aren't they speaking? I started thinking about this one day and an idea for a story began to take shape.

Phones are great. They are useful and fun. But the signal from our mobile phones can be used to track us. What if the person – or thing – at the other end of the line is evil and knows where we are ...?

To Rita Price and Maria Austin

Contents

1   A Phone to Die For   1

2   Telling Tales   7

3   The Goat Man   13

4   Something in the Darkness   17

5   The Creature on the Roof   25

6   Going Crazy?   29

7   Something Wrong   35

8   The Time Is Nearly Up   43

9   Leave Me Alone!   50

10   Halloween   57

11   A Long Way Home   68

12   Race Against Time   72

13   Too Late?   79

14   Payback   84

Chapter 1

A Phone to Die For

The mobile phone was lying on a red cloth in the boot of the car.

It was the only thing the man had for sale. He was young – about 22 – but his face was thin and pale and he had dark rings round his eyes. He looked ill and a bit scary, so Ryan just gave the phone a quick glance as he walked by. It was beautiful – a gold colour and with a huge screen.

Ryan spent over half an hour walking up and down looking at all the things people had for sale. The car boots and the stalls were

1

mostly filled with junk, and he kept thinking about that mobile phone. He was sure it was sold by now.

But when he went back, it was still there. And this time Ryan stopped. The day was quite warm, but the man was hunched up as if he was cold and his hand shook as he pointed to the phone.

"It's a bargain, mate. It's amazing. Got voice control. Picks up TV. Music and video download. Satellite tracking. It's got things like ... things like you've never seen."

The man's voice began to tremble, as if he was going to cry. His eyes were small and dark and he looked scared. Ryan wondered if he was on drugs or if the phone was stolen.

"How much?" he asked.

"Thirty?" the man said.

"Thirty?" Ryan said in surprise, thinking that it would be at least £100.

"OK – twenty," the man said.

Now Ryan was sure the phone was stolen so he shook his head and turned to go. But the man grabbed his arm.

"Ten, then. Take a look at it – you'll love it. Go on – pick it up. Play with it."

Ryan bent and picked the phone up. A small electric shock ran up his arm. The phone glowed warmly in his hand. It felt great.

"How do you turn it on?" he asked, holding it out.

The man put his hands behind his back as if he didn't want to touch the phone.

"It's all voice controlled. Just say 'Open' or 'Close' to turn it on and off."

"Open," Ryan said.

There was a burst of light on the screen and for a split second he thought he saw a strange face, but it was gone before he could be sure. Then letters and numbers swirled around the screen until they suddenly came together to read DIAVOLO 666.

"Just ask for whatever you want," the man said. "Phone, TV, video – and it goes straight there. You load your address book by voice and select calls by voice. It's simple. No charger needed – it charges itself. Solar power, I think. Texts and calls are free – DIAVOLO have their own network."

"TV," Ryan said, and the screen switched and came up with a list of channels. He selected one and spoke the name, "Sat Movie."

The screen switched and a movie was playing on the screen. It looked like a horror film.

"See? It's a phone to die for," the man said, darting a nervous look at the screen. "Come on, make up your mind – I've got to go."

"Ten, you said?"

"Yeah, ten's fine."

A shiver of doubt ran through Ryan, but then he took a £10 note out of his back pocket and handed it over.

"Is there anything else I need to know?" Ryan asked, but the man had already slammed his boot shut and was almost running to the front of the car. He got in and locked the door. A moment later the car was bumping across the field towards the exit. The car turned the corner and the scared young man was gone.

Ryan looked down at the screen.

The movie had stopped. In its place, in large bright letters, were the words "*Welcome, Ryan*".

It was so cool that it made him smile. Then it hit him. How could the phone know his name?

Something ran from his nose and a big drop of blood splashed down onto his hand.

Then another hit his shoe. And another splattered onto the ground.

Chapter 2
Telling Tales

His mum was still at work when Ryan got home. Her boyfriend, Colin, was in the hall-way putting down some new floor-boards.

"Mind where you step, mate," Colin said in a stupid Australian accent. "You'll have to do your old kangaroo jump."

"You're so funny – not!" Ryan snapped as he stepped over the gap in the floor-boards.

Colin had always put up with his insults before, so it took Ryan by surprise when the big man stood up and blocked his way to the stairs. Had he pushed him too far?

But Colin's voice was calm when he spoke. "Listen, I know how you feel. You're thinking, *Why do I have to put up with this guy in my house? I didn't choose him. I wish my dad was here.* But the fact is, your dad walked out on you six years ago, Ryan, and he's never made any effort to contact you. I know how hard that must be for you. But I'm not a bad guy. I've been living here for five months now – isn't it time we tried to get along? I really like you and I think we could be friends."

Ryan looked him in the eye and sneered, "Oh, yeah? Well, think again." Then he stepped past him and went upstairs to his room.

He was shaking with anger. How dare that creep talk about his dad like that? He reached behind the cupboard and pulled out the photo he had hidden there. Even after all this time he always got a stab of pain in his heart when he looked at it. His dad was standing next to his mum on a beach and they were both smiling in the sunshine. If only it could be like that again.

He put the photo back and pulled the DIAVOLO out of his pocket. It was such an amazing phone that, for one crazy moment, he felt as if he might find his dad's number on it and be able to speak to him again. Mad.

"Open," he said, and the beautiful phone came alive.

The letters and numbers swirled and formed the logo, DIAVOLO 666. Then the *Welcome, Ryan* screen opened.

He lay on his bed and started to load his address book, then he said, "Brandon," and sure enough the phone found the number and began calling it. Brandon's phone was engaged. And so was Adam's. Maybe they were talking to each other. Jamal's phone was turned off.

The only one of his friends who answered was Harry.

"Hey, Ryan – what's up?"

"Trying out my new phone."

"Cool. This your new number, then?"

"Yeah," said Ryan.

"OK, I've got it. I'm watching a DVD. Catch you later."

Ryan ended the call, looked through the menu and chose TV. A list of the channels came up and he selected one he hadn't heard of – "Diavolo Special". He almost dropped the phone as the screen filled with a porn movie. The girl was really pretty and he couldn't take his eyes off her. Then, suddenly, the man hit her and knocked her to the floor. She had tears in her eyes and she started to scream as the man threw himself on her. It was horrible, but he was still watching it when his door suddenly opened. He jumped in shock as his mum came into the room.

"Close!" he said quickly, and the phone closed down.

"What're you doing?" his mum asked.

"Just playing with my new phone," he said, holding it up. "Isn't it great? I got it at the car boot sale. Only ten quid."

"That's cheap," his mum said as she sat next to him.

"How was work?" he asked, hoping she wouldn't go into too much detail about the hospital. Sometimes she told him about all the terrible things that happened on the cancer ward where she was a nurse, and he hated having to listen to the stories of illness.

"Oh, rushed off our feet, as always," she said. "Ryan ..."

"What?"

She sighed. "I hear you've been rude to Colin, again."

"Ah, little baby been crying and telling tales, has he?"

"Honest, Ryan, I don't get you. You never used to be like this."

"It's him! He's pathetic, Mum! He drives me nuts with his stupid jokes all the time. And he's taken over everything. Always doing things on the house and cooking and stuff."

"I'm glad he does. You never help me with jobs around the house – you never have."

"It's our place – not his!" Ryan shouted and he could feel stupid tears coming to his eyes.

"It's soon going to be his, too," his mum said, walking to the door. She turned. "He's asked me to marry him and I've said yes."

Chapter 3
The Goat Man

Ryan woke with a start in the middle of the night. There was a strange buzzing noise coming from beside his bed. He rolled over and picked up the phone. The screen was flashing on and off so fast that he couldn't make out what it was showing. A face? Yes, a strange face. Man? Goat? Goat-man?

Then, in the flashing light, something moved on the top of the cupboard and his heart jerked with shock. A dark shape. A dark, dark shape, darker than the night. There. Gone. There. Gone.

He shot backwards and dropped the phone in terror. The light stopped flashing, leaving him in total darkness. There was a noise like the flapping of wings and a blast of cold air blew across his face. Ryan froze.

Silence.

No sound of wings.

Silence.

Just the knocking of his heart.

Silence.

Finally he reached out for the light next to his bed. It flashed on and he looked round. Nothing. No dark shape. Nothing.

And on the top of the cupboard just a pile of magazines and the black and white floppy hat his dad had bought him at a football match. By the side of the bed, the phone lay on the floor where he'd put it before he went to sleep. No flashing light. No strange face on the screen.

He lay for a while with the light on. Nothing. Everything perfectly normal. He switched off the light.

As he slipped back into sleep, the dream began.

Someone had stolen his phone. He tracked down the thief to an old hut near a river. There was a terrible row and he lost his temper and picked up a hammer. Blood and bits of bone flew through the air and splashed all over him as he smashed the hammer down onto the thief's head.

Ryan woke up with a jolt to feel his heart juddering and his body drenched in sweat.

The door burst open and he was blinded as the bedroom light flashed on. He blinked and saw his mum standing by his bed.

"Ryan, what is it?" she said. "You were screaming the house down."

"I was having a nightmare."

"What was it, love? Tell me."

"I can't remember. It was just horrible."

"Well, it's over now. Try to get to sleep again."

He lay back down and she tucked him in and gave him a kiss on his cheek the way she used to when he was a little kid. It was good to feel his mum's love again. But the instant she went out and closed the door, the horror came back. He'd said he couldn't remember the dream. But that was a lie. He could remember everything – the hammer, the blood, the bone. And, most terrible of all, he could remember the face of the person he had beaten to death.

It was Colin.

Chapter 4

Something in the Darkness

All his friends loved the DIAVOLO phone when he showed it to them at school.

"No top-ups? No contract? You sure?" Harry asked.

"That's what the guy said," Ryan replied.

"It's cool," Jamal said. "Why would he sell it for ten quid?"

It was a question that Ryan had asked himself a lot.

"I bet it was nicked," Brandon said.

Ryan nodded. But he didn't really believe it. He couldn't forget that haunted look in the man's eyes – as if he wanted to get as far away from the phone as he could.

"Why won't it do this voice control thing for me?" Adam asked.

"I don't know – maybe it only works for the owner. What do you want?"

"TV – Sky Sports," Harry said.

Ryan said the words and then handed the phone to Harry.

"Hey, that's so cool," Harry said. "Great picture, too. Oh, no, it's going all ... Wow, look at her! She's hot! Look at this porn, lads!"

Ryan saw that the channel had switched to "Diavolo Special". Everyone crowded round to look but Ryan said, "Close," and the phone shut down.

"Hey, put it back on!" Harry shouted but Ryan grabbed the DIAVOLO and put it in his pocket.

From then on, it seemed as if the phone had a mind of its own. Or, even more scary than that – it seemed to know what he was thinking. If he was watching a TV show and he thought about football, the phone would suddenly switch to a channel showing football.

The channel it switched to most was "Diavolo Special". He only had to fancy one of the girls on a TV show and the screen would fill up with a porn movie. And the scenes on that channel always started sexy but then became more and more violent. And no matter how horrible it became, he couldn't stop watching. Night after night he sat in his bedroom with the door locked – it was ugly and disgusting but it excited him.

And whenever he told the phone to close at the end of the evening, strange messages appeared just before the screen shut down. Messages he couldn't understand. One night it was "*Everything has a price.*" The next it was "*The contract is sealed.*" Another time it read "*Live now, pay later.*"

Did it mean that the man had lied and he would have to start paying rental every month? It was bound to be a lot of money for a phone with all these special features. It had everything. A brilliant camera. Email. Broadband. SatNav. It even had a feature called "Sat Spy" – you chose a post code or someone's mobile number and you could see live pictures from about five hundred feet in the air. He typed in his friends' phone numbers and he could see where they were. Maybe he could even follow them and see what they were doing – that was why it was called Spy. He'd have to try it one day.

It was a great phone, and he would hate to have to get rid of it because it cost too much to run.

Then one evening he had another row with Colin and he went upstairs feeling angry. He started watching a comedy show but it switched to "Diavolo Special" and the channel was showing footage of killings from all over the world. Close-ups of people begging for their lives before someone shot them or cut their throat. Terrorists blowing themselves up. Groups of soldiers torturing men and women.

The first evening, Ryan only watched it for five minutes then quickly turned it off. But the next evening he watched it again for longer. And the evening after that he watched for longer. Until he was watching it nearly all the time. Porn and violence. Porn and violence. He hated it but he couldn't stop.

"What do you do in your room every evening?" his mum asked, and Ryan looked away – he'd be so ashamed if his mum knew.

"Nothing. Homework and stuff," he lied.

Then the phone started turning itself on.

One night he closed it and went to sleep. Then once again a flashing light woke him. He reached over and felt for his phone.

There was the goat-man. He had slits for eyes, two horns on the head, a long, pointed chin and a twisted nose. His mouth was just a wide red gash. Then the picture changed and there was something else – something with wings. A dragon? A dinosaur? Ryan had never seen anything like it. There were flaps on either side of its head, a long snout and rows of sharp, pointed teeth. Then the screen went black and he was in darkness again.

And in that darkness he knew he was not alone. There was no noise, no movement, but something was there. Something that was alive. It was very close and it was staring at him.

He lay very still, hardly able to breathe. He tried not to panic. He tried not to scream. Then, finally, as if someone had walked out of the room, the thing was gone. He knew he was alone again. He rolled off the bed and staggered towards the door.

He got to his mum's bedroom and reached for the handle. Then he stopped. He hadn't woken her since Colin had moved in and he didn't want to start now. It would make him look like a little kid. And he didn't want to see them together in bed.

He tip-toed back to his room and switched the light on. Nothing. It all seemed normal but he couldn't forget the feeling of terror he had felt in the darkness.

He checked the phone: it was off. He got into bed, and left the light on. It was stupid, it was like being a baby, but he didn't care – it made him feel safer.

The next morning when he turned the phone on, the DIAVOLO logo wasn't there. Instead there was the face of the goat-man.

It stared at him. He tried to get rid of it but it wouldn't go. It stayed there and stared at him.

Chapter 5
The Creature on the Roof

Every time he looked at the phone, the face of the goat-man was there. The man's slitted eyes stared at Ryan as if they were trying to burn their way into his head. He could see that grinning face even when he wasn't looking at it, so it was a shock when the picture suddenly changed.

One morning the number 23 appeared underneath the face.

The next day it said 2355.

The day after, it read 235531.

Then a day later the figures 10 were added.

And that was where it stopped – 23553110.

Ryan wondered if it was a telephone number, so he rang it, but got a voice saying, "You have dialled an incorrect number. Please check the number and dial again."

He spent hours looking at the numbers, trying to work out what they meant, but he couldn't make sense of them. A couple of days later he turned the phone on and, instead of the usual letters and numbers swirling round and making DIAVOLO 666, he got C-B-Y-A-P-K-A, which rearranged themselves into the word "PAYBACK" above the numbers 23553110.

Payback. That must mean the phone wasn't free after all, and that he'd have to pay for it.

One evening after school he went to The Pines Shopping Centre with Harry. They looked at some shops, then went to a Burger King for fries and a Coke.

"Let's have a look at that porn channel," Harry begged.

"Get out of here, you pervert," Ryan laughed. "It's all you can think of!"

But the moment he said it, he realised that it wasn't Harry who couldn't think of anything else. It was him.

They split up and Ryan went towards the side exit of the mall. As he went out through the doors he lifted his head and caught a movement at the top of the office building across the street. It was nearly dark and it was too high to see clearly but ... was that a figure standing on the roof?

Something about the shape reminded him of the creature he'd seen, or thought he'd seen, on the cupboard in his bedroom. But this shape was bigger, much bigger. And its head looked like that dragon or dinosaur he'd seen on the phone, the one with all those sharp teeth.

Up in the sky, a flock of birds flew across the top of the building. They were starlings. Suddenly the creature darted up and caught two of them in its claws. It landed back on the roof, folded its wings, and bit the heads off the birds. Feathers burst into the air and floated down, swirling in the wind.

Ryan turned around but nobody else seemed to have noticed. When he looked back at the roof it was empty. The creature had gone.

Chapter 6
Going Crazy?

Two days later he saw the flying creature when he was coming out of school with his friends. It was sitting on the roof of a house opposite the school. And this time there could be no mistake – it was the same creature he'd seen on the phone. But so big! Big, big body and wings like leather. It opened its long jaw and he could see the rows of sharp, pointed teeth. He stood still in shock while the others went on walking.

"Hey, look!" he shouted.

The others turned round.

"What?" Brandon called.

Ryan looked. The creature had gone.

He felt weak, as if he was going to faint. What was happening – was he going crazy?

"Maybe it was some kind of bird of prey," his mum said that evening when Ryan tried to explain what he'd seen.

"A hawk," Colin suggested. "I read in the paper that they're coming back into city centres."

"You know everything, don't you?" Ryan sneered. "You geek!"

"Hey, stop it. You can go to bed if you're going to be like that," his mum snapped. "Go on – upstairs."

"Yeah, that's right – take his side."

"Ryan, I'm warning you. Upstairs. Now!"

Very slowly, just to annoy her, he got up and walked across the room. As he opened the door he turned back and saw Colin looking at him.

"God, I hate your guts!" Ryan shouted, then slammed the door behind him.

Stupid, stupid, stupid! As soon as he got up to his room he knew he'd acted like an idiot. All he'd done was push his mum away from him and closer to Colin. Stupid, stupid, stupid. Why couldn't he keep his mouth shut?

Maybe his mum was right – maybe he was different now. Maybe he was going crazy – seeing weird things, losing his temper, watching those TV channels.

The minute he thought about the TV programmes he wanted to watch one. He locked his door and went online.

At the end of the evening he told the phone to close and, as usual, a message came up.

"I'm yours, you're mine", it said, and Ryan felt a strange thrill. Yes, that was what it felt like – the phone was becoming part of him. He loved it.

The message faded and there was a quick flash of something else. It might have been the picture of that weird creature, but it was gone before he could be sure.

He reached over to switch the bedside light off then decided against it. He felt such a baby, but he didn't like sleeping in the dark any more.

****

"Hey, what's this habit of leaving your light on all night?" his mum asked the next day.

"Just prefer it," he said.

He could see that she was going to ask why, but Colin saved him by saying, "That's funny, I can remember when I was about fourteen I kept the light on all the time, too. I used to get these, like, panic attacks."

"Did you, Colin?" his mum said, then looked at Ryan. "You're not having those, are you?"

He shook his head and she started reading the paper. Colin gave him a quick look and a very slight nod, then went back to reading his *Train* magazine.

Ryan kept thinking about what Colin had said, and when his mum went upstairs for a bath he asked, "Did you really? Sleep with the light on?"

"Yep," said Colin.

"And you had panic attacks? What about?"

"I dunno – about dying, I suppose. I was 14 – all the changes going on. My body. My feelings. I realised that one day the big change was going to come – I was going to die. It kind of freaked me out."

33

Ryan thought about it. Maybe that was what was happening to him. Maybe he wasn't going crazy. Maybe everyone got panic attacks and had weird thoughts and weird dreams.

"It's not easy, growing up," Colin said. "I remember, sometimes I felt like I didn't know who I was any more. You know what I mean?"

Ryan nodded.

It felt strange – for the first time ever he didn't hate Colin.

Chapter 7
Something Wrong

Adam was the one who came up with the idea of having a party during the half-term holiday.

"My dad's going up to Scotland to visit my nan and he said I can have a few mates round as long as the house is clean when he gets back," Adam said. "Like he'd notice – the place is a tip since my mum left."

"So how many people are coming to this party?" Jamal asked.

"As many as we can cram in my house!"

"Girls, too?" Brandon asked.

"Of course girls!" Adam said.

So the half-term holiday started. The weekend was good because his mum and Colin were at home. On the Saturday afternoon they went to a fair to raise money for his mum's hospital. She was running a stall, selling old books and toys, and Colin and Ryan helped her.

"It's a flipping disgrace," his mum said as they set up the stall. "Having to do stuff like this to buy things that save people's lives. It's what our taxes ought to pay for, not weapons and wars."

"I know what you mean," Colin said. "But it's great to see all these people getting together to help and give money. It restores your faith in human beings."

"Oh, Colin," his mum smiled. "That's what I love about you. Always thinking positive."

It was raining on Sunday afternoon so Colin decided to take them to the cinema and then stop for a meal on the way home. It was a good film and they ate at King Pizza. It was Ryan's favourite restaurant, because the pizzas were huge and the ice cream was the best in town. So the weekend was a really good start to the holiday.

But the next day, Ryan woke up and knew at once that the house was empty. Of course, it was Monday and his mum and Colin must have left for work. He tried to go back to sleep but after a few minutes he started to feel that something wasn't right.

He got out of bed but the creepy feeling didn't go away. If anything, it got worse.

He stepped into the shower and let the hot water pour down onto him. Then, as he reached for the soap, he thought he heard a noise. He stood still and listened, but the splattering of the shower was loud so he switched it off.

There was silence, then a few drips.

The shower door was fogged up with steam so he couldn't see out. He held his breath to hear better. Then a terrible thought came into his head – someone was in the bathroom. Someone was out there.

He rubbed his hand over the glass and peered out.

No one.

But now he was too scared to stay in the shower so he quickly dried himself, got dressed, and went downstairs to the kitchen. He turned on the radio but the cheerful music didn't stop him feeling scared. He ate his breakfast and told himself that he was just being stupid but he wished his mum was at home. Or Colin. Yes, even him – Colin would tell him it was just a panic attack and not to worry.

After breakfast he made himself go back up to his room. He picked up his DIAVOLO and called Brandon and Jamal but neither of them answered. He left messages for them then he went on-line and tuned in to "Sat Spy".

Suddenly he had an idea and he typed in that strange number – 23553110. Perhaps it was like a post code. Normally "Sat Spy" started with a picture of the turning Earth but this time the screen went black. And out of the blackness there came a noise. It was soft at first but it grew louder and louder, until the hairs on his arms and neck stood up as he realised what it sounded like – a crowd of screaming people.

The noise filled the room but he knew the people weren't near – they were far, far away. The noise was only loud because there were millions of people and they were screaming at the tops of their voices.

"Close!" he shouted at the phone.

For one moment he thought it wouldn't work and that terrible sound would go on and on. Then the screen lit up with that grinning face of the goat-man and the DIAVOLO switched itself off.

The house was dead silent.

And suddenly he was too scared to stay there. He grabbed his jacket and flew down the stairs. He opened the door and ran out of the house, down the path and into the road.

He kept going until he came to the busy High Street. There were cars and people and noise and at last he stopped running. It was all ordinary and safe.

But he didn't want to go back home. Not yet. He didn't want to be alone – he wanted to be with people. So he went to The Pines

Shopping Centre. He spent ages looking at the shops and then bought a burger. In the end he stayed for over five hours and only went home when he was sure his mum and Colin would be back from work.

"Hey, I'm going to a party on Saturday evening," his mum said while they were all eating. "One of the doctors is going off to Australia so we're having a get-together to say goodbye."

"I'm going to one, too," Ryan said. "It's a Halloween party at Adam's."

"Oh, are you?" his mum said. "First I've heard of it. What time will you be back?"

"Me and everyone are staying over at Adam's."

"Oh, no, you're not. An all-night party? No way."

"It's not all night. We'll just all sleep over. Adam's dad says it's OK."

"Well, I say it's not."

"Oh come on, Mum – it's not fair. All my mates are going."

"No."

"You know what –?" Colin said.

Ryan was just about to tell him to get lost, but Colin went on, "I think he should go."

"What?" his mum said. "He's fourteen, Colin. I don't want him getting out of his head on drink and drugs at some party."

"Come on, Jenny. He's a sensible guy. He's not going to do anything stupid. I think you should trust him."

"I don't know," his mum said. But when Colin flashed a big smile at her, she couldn't help smiling back. "Oh, OK, then. But you promise – no alcohol, no drugs."

"Promise," Ryan said.

Chapter 8
The Time Is Nearly Up

The next morning he woke up very late. He got out of bed and heard the same scary silence in the house.

There was no sound, not a single sound, and yet it felt as if he wasn't alone – as if someone was there, someone holding their breath and making no noise.

He went down into the kitchen and put some cereal into a bowl, then opened the fridge to get the milk. As he turned back to the table his eye caught a movement in the doorway. Someone was standing there. He gasped in shock and dropped the milk.

He looked again and saw that the doorway was empty. A shadow. A coat hanging in the hall. That was all. His stupid brain playing tricks again.

Or was it?

He started cleaning up the spilt milk but he kept feeling shivers across his back and he couldn't stop himself from turning round and checking the doorway.

He had just finished mopping up the milk when the phone rang. He picked it up to see who it was, but there was no number on the screen.

"Hello?" he said

There was a long silence but he knew someone was there. Then came the voice. A soft, low whisper full of hissing menace.

"The time is nearly up."

The line went dead.

He couldn't take any more. He dashed out of the room, leaving his breakfast on the table. He grabbed his jacket and, for the second day in a row, he ran out of the house.

He went to the park and watched some young kids playing football. They seemed so happy and full of life and he felt cut off from them, as if he was standing behind a thick plate glass window. The silence and fear had followed him here.

He caught a bus and went to The Pines. He was wandering along one of the malls when he looked up at the people on the escalator and saw the young man who'd sold him the phone.

Ryan's heart jerked with shock. Maybe he was coming to take the phone back. No! He wouldn't let him. It was beautiful. It could do so many things. *"I'm yours, you're mine."* That was what it had said and it was true.

Then, as the young man got closer, Ryan saw it wasn't him after all.

He let out a sigh. It would be terrible to lose the DIAVOLO 666. But, on the other hand, he knew he didn't want more scary phone calls or strange messages.

That one this morning – *"The time is nearly up"* – what did that mean? Some kind of warning sent out by the company to tell him that he would have to start paying?

No, it was something more than that.

"The time is nearly up."

What time? His time!

His time was nearly up!

A cold terror squeezed his heart as the meaning of the message burst into his brain. He was going to die.

46

Soon, something terrible was going to happen to him and he would die.

He felt weak.

He was going to die. Die!

What would it be like? You would be alone, totally alone – nobody would be able to help, and nobody could die for you. It was you and you alone.

Was it painful to die? Of course, it must be. The lungs gasping for air. The heart stopping. The blood stopping. Sight going. Hearing going. The brain shutting down. It would be terrible, knowing it was the end.

And then what? Nothing? Endless nothing? Or was there life after death? Another world? Would God be there to judge him and send him to heaven or to hell?

He thought about his life. Had he sinned? What was a sin? What did it say in the Bible? Murder. Stealing. Something about being bad to people. Having to honour your father and mother. The Ten Commandments. Was he a sinner?

Fourteen. He was only fourteen. He couldn't die yet. His life had only just started. All those things he would never get the chance to do. All the things he would never know. The good times. Girls. Love. His friends would live on and he would be in the grave. Cold. Alone. Eaten by worms.

"You all right, son?" Ryan looked up at the security guard, looming over him.

"Yeah," he managed to say, though his voice sounded thick.

"You been drinking or something?"

"No."

"Well, you can't sit here all day, so you'd better move on."

Ryan's legs shook as he stood up but he forced himself to turn and walk to the exit.

Outside on the street the wind blew stinging rain into his face and it was like waking up from a bad dream. He looked at his watch – nearly four o'clock. He'd been sitting in the mall for hours – just staring at nothing, his head filled with thoughts of death. No wonder the guard had thought he looked strange.

But now he'd snapped out of it. He was alive. He wasn't going to die. It had just been a panic attack. Yes, that was it – a panic attack, like the ones Colin used to have.

He walked all the way home, letting the cold wind blow all the terror out of him, and letting the rain wash away his fears. And he was glad to see that there were lights on when he got home. He didn't want to be alone in an empty house.

Chapter 9
Leave Me Alone!

His mum wasn't going to work until the afternoon on Wednesday and he was glad he wouldn't be alone in the house. When he went into the kitchen she was cooking a meal and he asked if she wanted any help.

"Yeah, great. Colin asked me to get the sauce ready for his famous lamb curry – he's left me instructions. Let's see," she said, checking the piece of paper. "Oh, that's something you could do – cut up these onions and fry them for a bit, and add some pepper and chilli powder. I'll get on with the meat."

The onions sizzled when he put them into the hot pan and a delicious smell rose up as he stirred them. The kitchen was warm and cosy and his mum was singing to herself while she worked. This was so much better than sitting in The Pines, worrying about dying.

"That's perfect," his mum said when he finished frying the onions. She took the pan and tipped them over the meat, then added the rest of the curry mixture. "OK, we can pop it in the fridge now." She paused then asked, "What's up, Rhino?"

"What d'you mean?" he said, surprised – she hadn't used that nick-name for ages.

"Dunno. You look so sad. You look like that all the time nowadays. What's going on? Is it something at school?"

"No."

"What, then? Are you still angry about Colin?"

"No, he's all right." He was amazed to hear himself say it.

A smile of relief flashed across her face then she stroked his hair and asked, "So, what is it, then?"

Ryan told her. Let it all pour out – all the thoughts he'd had at the shopping centre.

"Come on, Ryan – you're not going to die."

"How do you know? You see young people die all the time in the hospital."

"That's because they're ill. You haven't got cancer – you're as healthy as anything. Stop worrying. Oh, come on, love," his mum said, putting her arm round him. "I hate to see you sad."

It was good to have her close like this but it made him feel embarrassed, too, and he pushed her arm away.

She turned back to the cooking and he could tell she was disappointed, so he went upstairs to his room and played video games until she called him down for lunch.

"Listen," she said while they were eating, "promise me you won't be stupid at this do of yours. No drinking, no smoking and *no* drugs."

"Oh, Mum, cut it out. You're always nag, nag, nag."

She flashed him an angry look and they finished the meal in silence.

Damn. It all felt wrong and he didn't know what to say to make it right again. She started to get ready for work and he hung around near the front door while she put on her coat.

"See you later," was all she said as she opened the door and stepped out into the cold, grey afternoon.

The moment she left the house, the DIAVOLO rang. He had down-loaded the ringtone because it had been his favourite song but now, hearing it playing upstairs, he hated it.

He thought of letting the phone ring and ring until it stopped, but he seemed to be drawn upstairs towards the sound. He opened the door to his bedroom and the ringing was louder than normal – like a baby crying, screaming and screaming to be picked up.

"Hello?" he said.

He knew it would be that voice again. That hissing voice. And he knew what it would whisper.

"The time is nearly up."

"Who are you?" he shouted. "Why are you doing this? Leave me alone!"

There was a noise at the other end – a cold little laugh – then the line went dead.

He threw the phone onto his bed and ran downstairs. He couldn't stay here. He'd go out. He'd go to The Pines again, where there would be crowds of people doing normal everyday things – chatting, laughing, doing their shopping.

He was putting his coat on when the front door banged open. He jumped in fright but it was Colin.

"Hey, Ryan! I'm glad you're here. I've taken this afternoon and tomorrow off work. I'm going to paint the spare room. Maybe you could give me a hand." He pulled two paint-brushes out of a paper bag and waved them in the air.

Ryan almost said no. Almost told him to stick his paint-brush where the sun doesn't shine. But he didn't. He said OK.

And it turned out to be good fun.

Colin played horrible music on his CD player and his jokes were as dumb as ever but Ryan tried not to listen. And they worked well together. By the time they finished late on Thursday afternoon the spare room looked great.

"Fantastic!" his mum said when she saw it. "You two should go into business together – Colin and Ryan, Master Painters."

Then Colin ruined it all by saying, "We could have a van – with Colin Beck and Son on the side."

"Get stuffed!" Ryan snapped. "I'm not your son – thank God."

And from there, it all went downhill and ended up with everyone shouting and angry.

Ryan stomped off to his room. He locked his door and spent the rest of the evening watching films of war and killing on "Diavolo Special".

Chapter 10

Halloween

He woke up on Friday morning feeling good. Nothing scary happened in the shower or while he was eating breakfast. There were no strange phone calls and all his fears seemed so stupid.

Of course he wasn't going to die. Of course he wasn't going mad. Of course there was nothing evil about the phone. Instead he turned it on and used the "Sat Spy" to check out where his friends were. He typed in their mobile numbers and saw that Brandon and

Jamal were both at the bowling alley, so he decided to go and meet up with them.

They played some video machines then had a couple of games of bowling. It was a good laugh and he was on top form and won both games with five strikes in the first game and six in the second.

"Here, what you going to the party as, Ryan?" Brandon asked in the café afterwards.

"Dunno. What about you?"

"A werewolf. I'll wear black jeans and a black T-shirt and I'm going to get a wolf mask from the joke shop in town. Jamal's going as a skeleton."

"Yeah, my brother bought it last year," Jamal said. "It's a bit big for me but it's great – it's got, like, a body suit with painted bones and a skull mask."

"Maybe I could go as a vampire," Ryan suggested.

"Yeah – you can buy some vampire teeth and fake blood at the joke shop," Brandon said. "We could meet up just before it closes then go on to the party together."

"OK."

"I can't wait – it's gonna be awesome!" Jamal said.

****

Ryan nearly had a row with his mum before he left the house on Saturday afternoon. She started nagging him, telling him that he ought to take a pair of pyjamas and a change of clothes. Then she started on again about drinking and drugs.

"How many times do I have to tell you?" he moaned. "I don't drink! I don't do drugs! And I don't need pyjamas, we're just going to sleep on the floor. I can change when I get back tomorrow."

"Oh, I don't know," she said, looking worried. "Still, I suppose Adam's dad will make sure everything's OK. Perhaps I should ring him, just to have a word."

"No!" Ryan shouted as she turned towards the phone.

"Why not?" she asked.

"Because you'll make me look an idiot, that's why," he said, blushing at his lie. If she rang and found out there wouldn't be any adults there, she'd never let him go.

"Oh, come on, Jenny," Colin said gently, coming to his rescue again. "It'll be all right. Let the boys have a bit of fun."

His mum let out a sigh. "Oh, well, I suppose you're right."

Ryan could see that she still wasn't sure, so he left the house early before she could change her mind.

He got to the joke shop and hung around waiting for Brandon. It was already dark and an old lady shuffled towards him wearing a long dirty coat and fluffy slippers. The left side of her face was covered with bruises and scabs and she was talking to herself. She stopped and grinned at him, showing a few broken teeth. She pointed at him, then went shuffling off down the street.

Brandon turned up at 5.15 and they went into the shop and bought their costumes, then caught the bus out to where Adam lived. His house was at the end of a long lane with fields on one side and only a few houses on the other. They stood outside and quickly changed into their costumes, then rang the doorbell.

The party was well under way. Music was pounding from the sound system and the house was packed with people dressed in weird costumes. There were monsters, devils, witches, aliens, zombies and lots of people wearing the *Scream* mask. Adam had covered himself with bandages and was walking round his house as if he was the Mummy, but the bandage had started to come off and people kept grabbing the end and pulling him.

The funniest costume was Jamal's skeleton. The skull mask looked good, but the body suit was way too big and all the white bone marks sagged together as if he was made of rubber.

Everybody had clubbed together for Adam to get drinks in and some people were already drunk. Ryan got a beer and drank it quickly, then went back and got another. Then someone offered him a swig of vodka and he took a long pull at the bottle.

He'd been telling his mum the truth when he'd said he didn't drink, and he found that the booze hit him quickly. His legs felt wobbly but he couldn't help smiling – all these monsters and ghosts were a laugh. He wasn't going to die. He was like all the other young people here – he was going to live and live and live. And he was going to have fun!

He went into the front room and joined in the dancing. The lights were off and everybody was just moving around, jumping and swaying and bumping into each other, and he jumped and swayed and bumped with them. He was wild and mad like all the other monsters and he danced and laughed and danced. And the music pounded in his head and he forgot everything.

After a bit he couldn't dance any more, and he made his way out into the hall-way and along to the kitchen.

"Ryan!" Harry shouted, and pushed through the crowd towards him with a bottle of wine. "Where've you been, man? God, you look really weird. I don't care – you're still my mate. Have a drink."

He held the bottle out but Ryan shook his head.

"Oh, well," Harry said, and took a couple of big swigs then staggered to the other side of the room.

Ryan found a plastic glass in the sink and filled it with water. He drank it, then filled it again and drank that, too. As he filled the glass for a third time he looked up at the clock on the wall and was shocked to see that it was already twenty to eleven. The time had flown.

He went back along the corridor and caught sight of himself in a mirror. No wonder Harry had said he looked weird. He'd put some of his mum's eye-liner round his eyes so that they would be dark like a vampire and he'd put fake blood round his mouth. All the dancing and sweating had made the colours run and his face was a mess of red and black.

He climbed the stairs to the bathroom. As he walked past the bedroom where he'd left his jacket he heard the ring tone of his phone but he wasn't going to answer the stupid thing. Let it ring until it stopped.

He washed all the mess off his face and peered into the mirror. Even though he had taken the make-up off, it hardly looked like him. Those dark, scared eyes. He was starting to look like the young man he had bought the phone from.

Someone banged loudly on the door and he went over and unlocked it.

Harry barged past him and bent over and threw up in the bath. Ryan dashed out of the door before the stench could hit him. He went to the top of the stairs and remembered his phone. It wasn't ringing any more, but maybe he should check who had called him.

He walked into the bedroom and found a girl from his class called Danielle Lester. She was holding his phone.

"It kept on ringing," she said. "So I answered it."

"Bloody hell – you've got a nerve."

"OK, OK – I'm sorry. All I did was answer it." She walked past him to the door. "Anyway, the phone's wrong."

"What?"

"The time's wrong. The date's right – the 31st of the 10th, but the time's wrong. It's 22.55, not 23.55."

"What are you talking about?" he asked, but she stepped out of the door and was gone.

He looked down at the phone. The 31st of the 10th what? And then, with a shudder he saw it, understood it. The 31st of October. Today. Halloween.

And the first two numbers were a time. 23.55. Five to midnight.

23553110: five to midnight on the 31st of October.

And that was what the voice on the phone had meant – *"The time's nearly up."* Payback.

In one hour's time – at five to midnight on the 31st of October – he would have to pay.

Chapter 11
A Long Way Home

He stood alone in Adam's bedroom, trying to tell himself it only meant he would have to start paying for the phone. But he didn't believe it.

Ever since that devil face had appeared, he had been scared. He'd tried to deny it but he couldn't deny it any more – at five to midnight something terrible was going to happen to him.

There were shouts and laughter from down below and the music boomed louder than ever. Most of his friends were drunk or busy dancing. He couldn't rely on them. He had to get home. Home, where people cared about him and would protect him.

He had to go. Now. While there was still time. If he got a bus he could be back home within half an hour and he would be safe.

He grabbed his jacket and ran down the stairs. Jamal and Brandon were standing near the open front door but he pushed past them.

"Hey, where you going?" Brandon called, but Ryan didn't answer.

He ran down the front path to the lane. It was dark, very dark – no street lights, no moon, no stars. The lane seemed empty. He took a deep breath and started running towards the lights of the main road. If he could just get there he would feel safer – there would be people and cars.

But it was a long, long way and panic surged up in him as he ran. Maybe something was hiding in the shadows. He couldn't hear anything above the sound of his stamping feet so he kept looking back, fearing that he would see someone – or something – come roaring out of the darkness behind him.

His heart was pounding hard and the cold air hurt his lungs. Keep going. Keep going. His legs were tired but he had to keep going.

At last he burst out on to the main road. He stopped next to the first lamp-post and bent over, hands on knees, trying to get his breath back.

He heard a few cars speed past but suddenly there was a deeper engine throb and he looked up to see a bus coming towards him. It was a 49 – the very one he needed.

The bus swept by and he turned and raced after it. There was a bus stop about 40 metres down the road and the brake lights of the bus glowed red as the driver slowed.

Ryan pushed himself harder, closing the gap. One last effort and he could jump aboard and the bus would take him home. Then the brake lights went out and he heard the engine note change as the driver saw that nobody was waiting at the stop.

"Wait!" Ryan screamed, but the bus pulled away, leaving him standing breathless and scared on the empty pavement next to the bus shelter.

Glass crunched under his feet and he saw that someone had smashed all the panels of the shelter and sprayed paint over the timetable so that he couldn't see how long he would have to wait for another bus.

Chapter 12
Race Against Time

The minutes ticked by.

He tried not to, but he kept checking his watch.

23.08.

23.09.

23.10.

Now he had just 45 minutes to get home.

He stared down the road, willing a bus to appear. Head-lights kept sweeping out of the darkness towards him but they all belonged to cars. Could he stick his thumb out and hitch a lift? No. Any kind of weirdo might stop and pick him up.

He could imagine being driven away to some lonely spot. Then what? A knife? Or some more terrible death? Tied up and tortured for days. Or buried alive.

23.12.

23.13.

And then it hit him. The phone! He'd got into such a panic that he'd completely forgotten that he could use it to ring his mum and get her to come and pick him up.

He was about to call home when he remembered – she wasn't there; she was out at her party. Never mind, he could ring Colin and ask him to come. No, his mum had got the car.

Wait a minute – maybe she'd taken her mobile. He said the words, "Mum's mobile," then put the phone to his ear and listened. It rang and rang, then the answer message came on.

He clicked "Disconnect" and the devil face grinned up at him while the warning "*Payback 23553110*" flashed faster and faster like a strobe light, sending his brain spinning. He tore his eyes away from it and looked up. A bus was coming.

"Make it a 49. Please make it a 49," he said out loud. But as it drew closer he could see that it was a 22. It went nowhere near his home.

But he stuck out his hand and the bus stopped. Better to be on the bus with other people than standing alone on the street.

"Where do you go in town?" he asked the driver.

"Old Wells Road. The Pines. Central Station."

"OK, the station."

He paid the fare and went and sat down.

If he got off at the station he could cut through Greenslate Industrial Estate and come out on Dyer Road. Once he was there he was nearly home.

He looked at his watch.

23.21.

It was going to be tight. Twenty minutes to get to the station, then ten minutes to cross the industrial estate. A few minutes along Dyer Road and home. He might just do it in time.

The bus started to grind up a hill towards the ring road. They crawled past the mosque and he checked his watch again.

23.25.

The bus came to a stop at the ring road and then sat there, the engine throbbing, waiting. The cars were coming so fast that the

driver didn't have time to pull out safely.
Come on! Come on!

23.26.

At last there was a break in the stream of
cars and the bus turned left onto the ring road.
And now it was speeding along. Lights flashed
by and Ryan began to hope again.

They turned off the ring road onto Old
Wells Road and soon he could see the tall
outline of The Pines ahead. They went round
the big roundabout and drew up in front of the
main entrance. The cinema must have just
shut, because a lot of people were waiting at
the stop.

One by one, oh, so slowly, they got on, paid
their fares and sat down.

The bus jerked and started off again. He
looked at his watch.

23.37.

They'd lost time. He wasn't going to make it.

And when they turned off Old Wells Road on to Station Road, there was a long line of stopped cars and, in front of them, the flashing blue light of an ambulance. A policeman was standing in the middle of the road directing the traffic.

The bus crept forward. Stopped. Crept forward. Stopped.

23.39.

23.40.

Ryan looked out of the window as they got closer to the ambulance. The paramedics were putting someone on a stretcher. There were broken bottles and blood on the pavement and a big crowd of people staring.

23.41.

The bus drew out and moved slowly past the ambulance then sped along Station Road, past the long row of pubs and clubs. Finally it arrived at the station car park. A crowd of young people was blocking the entrance. There was an argument going on and nobody moved when the driver flashed his lights at them.

"Come on, you drunken yobs – move!" the driver grumbled.

"I'll get off here," Ryan called, getting up and standing by the door.

"Look at them. Worse than animals," the driver muttered as a fight broke out. "OK, I'd better drop you off here."

He pressed a button, the doors opened with a hiss, and Ryan stepped off the bus.

Chapter 13

Too Late?

Ryan dodged round the edge of the fighting crowd and ran across the car park. He dashed down the dark alleyway by the side of the station and up the stairs to the footbridge. He was nearly across when a high-speed train screamed underneath, rattling the bridge.

He reached the far side and jumped down the steps, two at a time, and almost fell when he hit the pavement.

He looked up the empty road ahead. A few street lamps stretched away into the distance, making little pools of light in the darkness.

And on either side of the road, nothing but warehouses and factories with security fences around them. No houses, no shops or pubs for nearly half a mile until he got to Dyer Road.

23.46.

Nine minutes left. He'd never make it in time, no matter how fast he ran. But he couldn't just stay here. He had to get as close as possible. Maybe Colin would come and meet him.

He reached for his phone and rang home.

Colin answered almost at once, "Hello?"

"Colin – it's me."

"Ryan. You at the party?"

"No, I'm in Greenslate Industrial Estate. Can you come and meet me? Please. Please."

"Of course. Stay there."

"No!" Ryan cried, terrified at the thought of waiting while the minutes sped by to 23.55. "I'll be coming along Dyer Road. I'll meet you half-way or something."

"OK. I'll leave at once."

"Please be quick!"

"Ryan, what's the matter? Tell me."

Colin sounded worried and Ryan suddenly realised that his stepfather-to-be really did care about him. Ryan's eyes filled with tears and his voice cracked as he said, "Colin, I'm scared."

"Don't be scared. I'm on my way – it'll be all right. OK? OK?"

"Yeah, OK," he said. He was about to click the phone off when he knew he had to say something. Just in case. Just in case he never got the chance. "Colin?"

"What?"

"I'm sorry ... about everything."

There, he'd said it.

"Ryan, don't be daft. You don't have to be sorry for anything. You're an ace kid and I really like you. Do you hear me?"

"Yeah."

"Good. Now get going. I'll see you in a minute."

Ryan closed the phone and began to run.

He raced past factories, warehouses and used car lots. Security lights flashed on as he ran, shining on rolls of razor wire on top of walls and fences.

He looked down at his watch.

23.51.

How far had he run? How far to go? Could that yellow glow in the sky be from the lights on Dyer Road?

Then, in the distance, against that glow, he saw something that froze his heart and made him stop in fear. A black shape took off from the roof of the factory and flew across the road to another roof.

Chapter 14
Payback

The creature flew along the line of the roofs towards him. Then Ryan lost sight of it against the dark night sky. But in the silence he could hear the flap of its large, leathery wings growing louder and louder.

Then they stopped.

Somewhere in the dark it had landed and was looking down at him like a wild beast watching its prey.

It had come for him. It was waiting for 23.55.

He burst away in panic, running for his life, a scream of terror stuck in his throat. Down the road, through the pools of light. The whole world jerking and jumping as he pushed his legs faster.

There, ahead of him, he could see the end of the industrial estate, could see the lights of Dyer Road. Another minute and he would be there.

But then he heard the flapping of those leather wings and he glanced over his shoulder to see where the creature was. Nothing. Just the sound.

He looked to the front again and saw the dark shape of a man standing directly in his path. He tried to dodge round him but the man darted to the side and blocked his way.

Ryan skidded to a stop and the man grabbed him and threw him hard against the fence. The wire mesh pushed him forward again, almost onto the point of the knife the man was holding out.

Ryan sucked in a huge gasp of air and raised his arms.

"Don't!" he panted. "Please!"

"Please!" the man mocked, waving the knife close to Ryan's face.

He wasn't that old, perhaps still in his twenties, but he looked terrible. His eyes were empty, their pupils huge and black, and they had enormous dark rings round them. There were sores on his forehead and a scar that ran from the side of his mouth down to the stubble on his chin.

The man blinked and rubbed his nose roughly. It was obvious he was high on something and Ryan knew he would be able to outrun him if he could just get past him. But that knife was too close and the man was too jumpy and edgy to risk making a sudden move.

"Give me your money!" the man ordered.

Ryan felt in his pockets and pulled out a note and a few coins.

"Is that it?" the man said, grabbing them and stuffing them into his coat.

"It's all I've got. Honest."

"Yeah!" the man sneered and put the tip of the knife on Ryan's throat. "You don't want me to stick you with this, you give me everything, right?"

A dirty, sickly smell hit Ryan as the man leaned in and started to feel his jacket.

"What's this?" he asked, tapping Ryan's pocket.

"My phone."

"Give it to me."

Ryan pulled it out and handed it to him.

"Nice," the man said, holding it in his hand and playing with the keys. "How do you turn it on?"

"Just say 'Open' – it's voice controlled."

"Open," the man said and he smiled with pleasure as the phone lit up. "Not bad. Not bad at all."

He laughed as he stared at the screen.

"Look at that – *'I'm yours, you're mine.'* Too right – it's mine now." The man quickly tapped Ryan's other pockets. "Nothing else?"

"No," Ryan said, noticing the drop of blood that had suddenly appeared at the end of the man's nose. It swelled and fell. The man ran his hand across his nose and looked at the blood in surprise.

"On your knees," the man said.

Ryan had no choice. He knelt down.

The man pressed the knife against the skin just below Ryan's ear. One push and the knife would slice into his neck.

Was this it? Was this how he would die? Pumping his blood into the gutter? Was this junkie the one who had been sent for payback?

"On your belly," the man ordered, and he pushed the back of Ryan's head until he was forced to lie flat.

Two drops of the man's blood splattered on the ground just in front of him.

"You stay there. Right? Follow me and I'll kill you."

Ryan saw the man turn away and start to run towards the lights of Dyer Road. It was a crazy, shuffling run, as if he had trouble staying on his feet.

Then came a loud, high-pitched whine.

The man stopped and looked down at his hand. The noise was coming from the phone. He shook it but the noise went on.

Ryan got up to his knees. What was happening?

The whine continued, louder than ever. The man raised the phone to throw it away, then changed his mind and shoved it into his pocket. He broke into his shuffling run again, heading for the bright lights of Dyer Road.

There was a leathery flapping noise and Ryan turned to see the creature flying towards him. He threw himself to the ground, covering the back of his head with his arms, and felt the rush of air as those big wings flapped over him.

He looked up, expecting to see the creature swing round and come at him again, but it was flying down the road, its sharp ears lifted as if it was following that high-pitched whine.

He looked at his watch and understood.

23.55.

The whine was the signal for payback.

The creature swooped lower, following the whining noise.

Ryan could see the man nearly at the end of the road. He was framed against the bright lights of Dyer Road. The man turned his head as he heard the creature behind him.

He froze in horror for a moment, then he tried to escape. He dodged from one side of the road to the other, then tried to double back on himself. But the creature wouldn't let him get away – it dived under him, twisting and turning, and pushing him forward.

Ryan could see what it was doing. It was driving the man out into Dyer Road. Out into the busy main road.

An instant later there was a scream of brakes and the man shot high into the air as a car hit him. His body turned cartwheels across the roof of the car then crashed onto the ground.

There was another scream of brakes and the wheels of a big van bumped over the man's head and dragged him along the road.

The flying creature circled high above, looking down, then flapped away into the night. Its job was done.

Ryan was on his feet, running.

He got to the end of the road and the bright lights dazzled him.

Car doors were opening. People were getting out. He heard voices.

"Oh, God – he came from nowhere. I didn't have time ..."

"I saw it. It wasn't your fault ..."

Ryan stared at the mess – the huge puddle of blood trickling across the road. The man's head split open and crushed almost flat. The broken body, lying in a lifeless heap.

There was a crackling sound and his eyes were drawn to something near the rear wheel of one of the cars.

It was the DIAVOLO 666, or what remained of it. It had been crushed by the impact. As he looked, Ryan saw a spark and a cloud of smoke. The next second the wires and the metal and the plastic began to curl up and melt into the tarmac.

"Ryan! Oh, God! Thank God!"

He turned to see Colin running towards him.

His stepfather-to-be stopped in front of him, his eyes wide and staring.

"You're all right," he said, his voice shaking. "You're all right!"

Ryan nodded and Colin took hold of his shoulders and pulled him into a hug.

"Oh, God, Ryan, I thought it was you. Oh, thank God you're safe."

He stepped back, letting Ryan go, and called, "Has someone rung the police?"

"They're on their way," one of the men said.

Ryan's eyes were seeing it all – the man talking, the two men bent over the body, the group of women standing near one of the cars – but it was remote, blocked off from where he could feel anything.

"Come on," he heard Colin say. "Let's go."

He let Colin turn him round and he made his feet move in that direction.

He heard Colin ask him again if he was all right and he made himself nod.

When at last he looked back, the cars and the people were already a long way behind them.

Far away he could hear a police car siren.

Colin put his arm round his shoulder and Ryan let it stay there, steady, comforting, loving.

"Nearly home," Colin said. "Nearly home."

Barrington Stoke would like to thank all its readers for commenting on the manuscript before publication and in particular:

Maddie Allen
Georgina Barningham
Finlay Bell
Paige Bradley
Richard Brant
Gemma Brooks
Molly Burndred
Paige Caldaralo
Sean Campbell
Jay Condliffe
Tom Currie
Jeanette Cutland
Luke Dry
Alfie Duke
Peter Duncan
Marcus Eagles
Jordan Edgecombe
Billy Elliott
Zen Etchells
Matthew Faulds
Susan Gillespie
Joe Griffiths
Fraser Grigor
Jack Ives
Asher Knight

Joe Knowles
Ashleigh Lamond
Louise MacKenzie
Josh Macmillan
Joe Malcom
Sean Manson
Ryan Marfleet
Alwyn Martin
Joseph Martin
Andrew Miller
Nathan Morgan
April Norfolk
Thomas Pearman
Darrio Platt
Hannah Reek
Rebecca Reid
Will Roberts
Zennor Robinson
Joanna Nicola Shand
Lorne Stoddart
Steven Urquhart
Rebekah White
Mark Williams
James Wright

Become a Consultant!

Would you like to give us feedback on our titles before they are published? Contact us at the email address below – we'd love to hear from you!

info@barringtonstoke.co.uk
www.barringtonstoke.co.uk